Captain AWESOME
HAS THE BEST SNOW DAY EVER?

By STAN KIRBY
Illustrated by GEORGE O'CONNOR

LITTLE SIMON
New York   London   Toronto   Sydney   New Delhi

This book is a work of fiction. Any references to historical events, real people, or real places are used fictitiously. Other names, characters, places, and events are products of the author's imagination, and any resemblance to actual events or places or persons, living or dead, is entirely coincidental.

LITTLE SIMON

An imprint of Simon & Schuster Children's Publishing Division • 1230 Avenue of the Americas, New York, New York 10020 • First Little Simon hardcover edition November 2016 • Copyright © 2016 by Simon & Schuster, Inc. All rights reserved, including the right of reproduction in whole or in part in any form. LITTLE SIMON is a registered trademark of Simon & Schuster, Inc., and associated colophon is a trademark of Simon & Schuster, Inc. For information about special discounts for bulk purchases, please contact Simon & Schuster Special Sales at 1-866-506-1949 or business@simonandschuster.com. The Simon & Schuster Speakers Bureau can bring authors to your live event. For more information or to book an event contact the Simon & Schuster Speakers Bureau at 1-866-248-3049 or visit our website at www.simonspeakers.com. Designed by Jay Colvin. The text of this book was set in Little Simon Gazette.

Manufactured in the United States of America 1016 FFG 10 9 8 7 6 5 4 3 2 1

Cataloging in Publication Data for this title is available from the Library of Congress.

ISBN 978-1-4814-7816-8 (hc)

ISBN 978-1-4814-7815-1 (pbk)

ISBN 978-1-4814-7817-5 (eBook)

Table of Contents

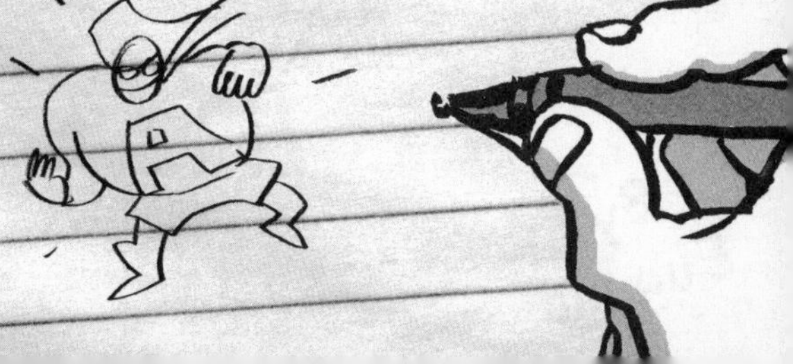

CHAPTER I

Weather or Not, Here We Come!

By
Eugene

If there was ever a worse thing for a teacher to say than, "Everyone, take out your math books," Eugene McGillicudy hadn't heard it.

Eugene reached into his desk and pulled out his math book. As he did, a folded square of paper fell out and dropped to the floor.

A NOTE.

Eugene looked around the room at his classmates. *Who sent*

me a note? he wondered.

Whenever Super Dude got a note, it was usually a secret message. A warning of evil! A clue!

What's that, you say? You've never heard of Super Dude?! Do you live on a space station orbiting Galaxian 459 on the other end of Black Hole 22? Super Dude is

only the greatest superhero in the
history of comic books! It was his
adventures that inspired Eugene to
become his *own* superhero, Captain
Awesome, the fighter of all that's
evil in Sunnyview. Then his best
friends joined him. Charlie Thomas
Jones was Nacho Cheese Man and
Sally Williams was Supersonic Sal.

Together, they were the Sunny-view Superhero Squad, protecting their school, their town, and the whole *universe* from evil.

And right now, Eugene was convinced that there was evil in this note. His Awesome Sense was tingling.

He began to unfold the piece of paper, but then stopped. Super Dude had once fought The Amazing Hypnotattler in Super Dude No. 48. The Amazing Hypnotattler's power lay in secret notes that hypnotized people into doing whatever the note said. Perhaps the Hypnotattler was hypnotizing superheroes in Sunny-view!

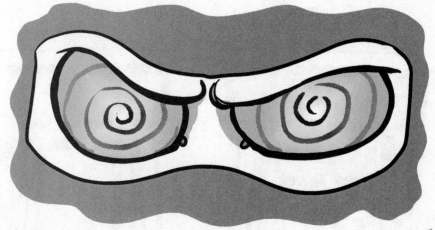

I have to get rid of this before anyone else reads it and falls under its spell, Eugene thought. He slid off his chair.

"Eugene, where are you going?" Charlie whispered. "Bathroom break

isn't for ten minutes." Charlie pointed to his watch. "I keep track."

"I've got to throw something away," Eugene whispered. "The Sunnyview Superhero Squad is in danger!"

"You'll get caught," Sally whispered back. "Ms. Beasley has Teacher Radar."

Ms. Beasley's back was to the class as she wrote on the whiteboard.

Eugene tip-tip-tiptoed toward the trash can.

"Where are you going, Eugene?" Ms. Beasley asked without turning around.

Eugene froze. *How does she do
that?!* he wondered.

When Ms. Beasley did turn
around, she said, "Is that a note in
your hand?"

Eugene gulped. "Y-y-yes."

"You know my rule about pass-ing notes," Ms. Beasley said.

Eugene's shoulders slumped as he placed the note in her hand and returned to his desk. It was all over now. The Hypnotattler had

won and there was nothing Eugene
could do to stop him.

Ms. Beasley carefully unfolded
the note. "'What did one pencil say
to the other?'" she read.

The whole class
leaned forward
in their seats,
wanting to know
the answer.

"'You're
looking sharp,'"
Ms. Beasley read.
"Oh my, that's
clever!"

The class burst into laughter, and even Eugene chuckled.

"I knew you'd like it, Eugene," whispered Sally. "But why were you trying to throw my joke away?"

"*Your* joke? *You* put it in my

notebook?" Eugene was shocked. "I thought it was an evil hypno-spell from the Hypnotattler."

Sally laughed. "Not everything is evil, Eugene."

RING!
RECESS TIME!

Ms. Beasley looked out the

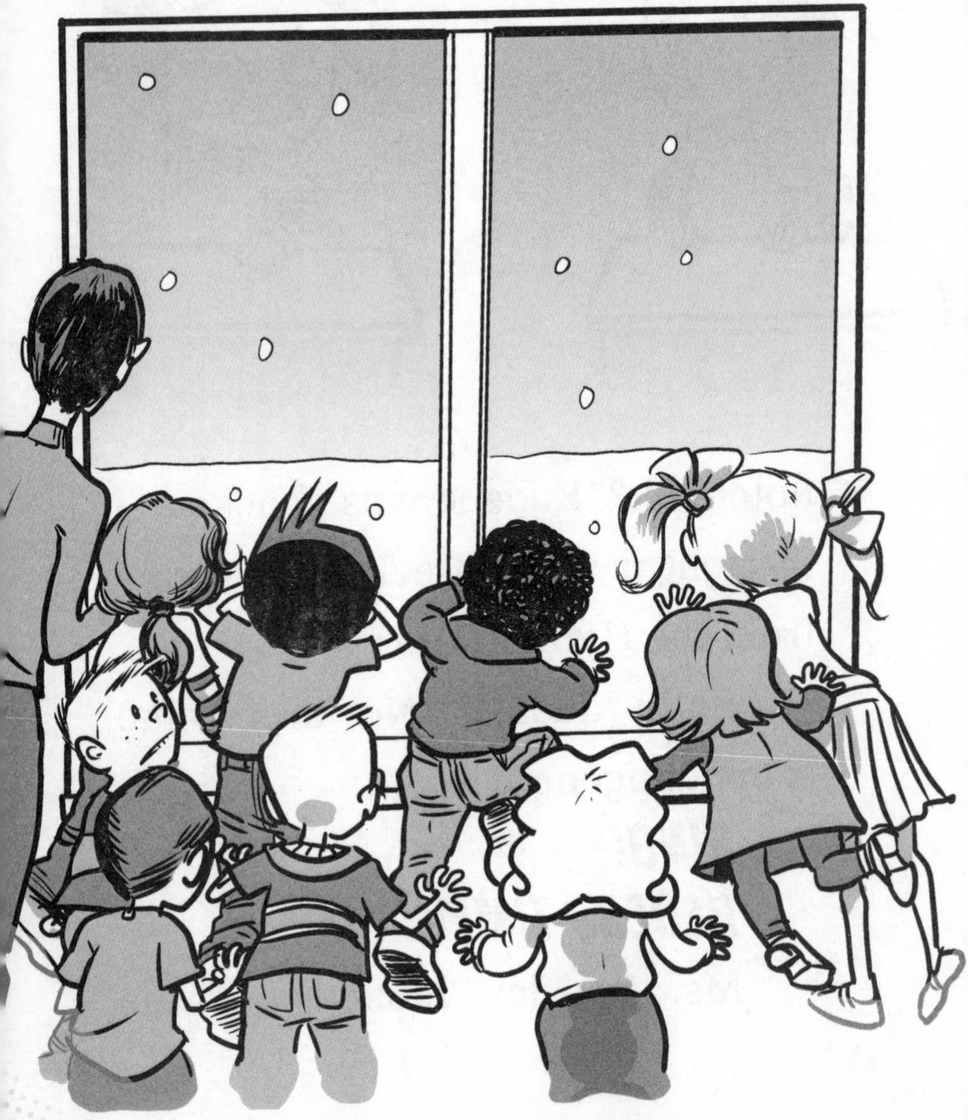

window. "Looks like we're going to have recess in the gym today, class."

Everyone excitedly ran to the windows and pressed their noses against the cold glass. Snow flurries fluttered across the playground.

"If this keeps up, maybe tomorrow will be a snow day!" Charlie said hopefully.

"Don't count on it," said Eugene. "Evil will make sure we're back in this classroom tomorrow."

CHAPTER 2

It Was
Quiet. Too
Quiet.

BY
Eugene

Abracadabra! Binny-Boom-Bop! Eugene waved his fingers over his vegetables. "Be gone, vegetables, be gone!"

"What are you doing, honey?" Eugene's mom asked.

"I'm trying to make these evil vegetables that are *disguised* as dessert disappear," he replied. "But my Captain Awesome pow-ers have failed me."

"It's just zucchini cake, Eugene," his mother replied. "And you can hardly taste the zucchini."

"But I can see the little green pieces in there, hiding, ready to leap out and take over my stom-ach," Eugene pointed out.

"Oh, I can make this disappear,"

said Eugene's dad. "I'll just use my Super Dad powers." Eugene's dad jabbed at the zucchini cake with his fork and took a bite. "Delicious!"

Score! Eugene thought. "Can I go upstairs now?" he asked his parents.

Mr. and Mrs. McGillicudy said he could as long as he brushed his teeth before getting into bed.

Eugene did as told. As Super Dude would have said, "Parents know best—usually." Then Eugene climbed into bed and settled in to read the *Super Dude Winter Spectacular No. 26.* He got to the part where Super Dude was about to battle the evil Elfenstein, and then—

ZZZZZZZZZZ.

He fell asleep.

• • •

The next morning, Eugene opened
one eye. It was quiet. Too quiet.
He opened his other eye.
He looked around.
His school clothes
weren't laid out on
his Super Dude chair.
He didn't hear
Queen Stinkypants
crying downstairs for
her breakfast. Eugene
rolled over and looked at his
Super Dude alarm clock.

8:30?

8:30!

Eugene gasped. Right now he should be avoiding Little Miss Stinky Pinky and racing to his desk.

What was going on? Could it be? No, it couldn't be . . .

Eugene ran to the window. It was!

SNOW!

And that meant only one thing: **SNOW DAY!**

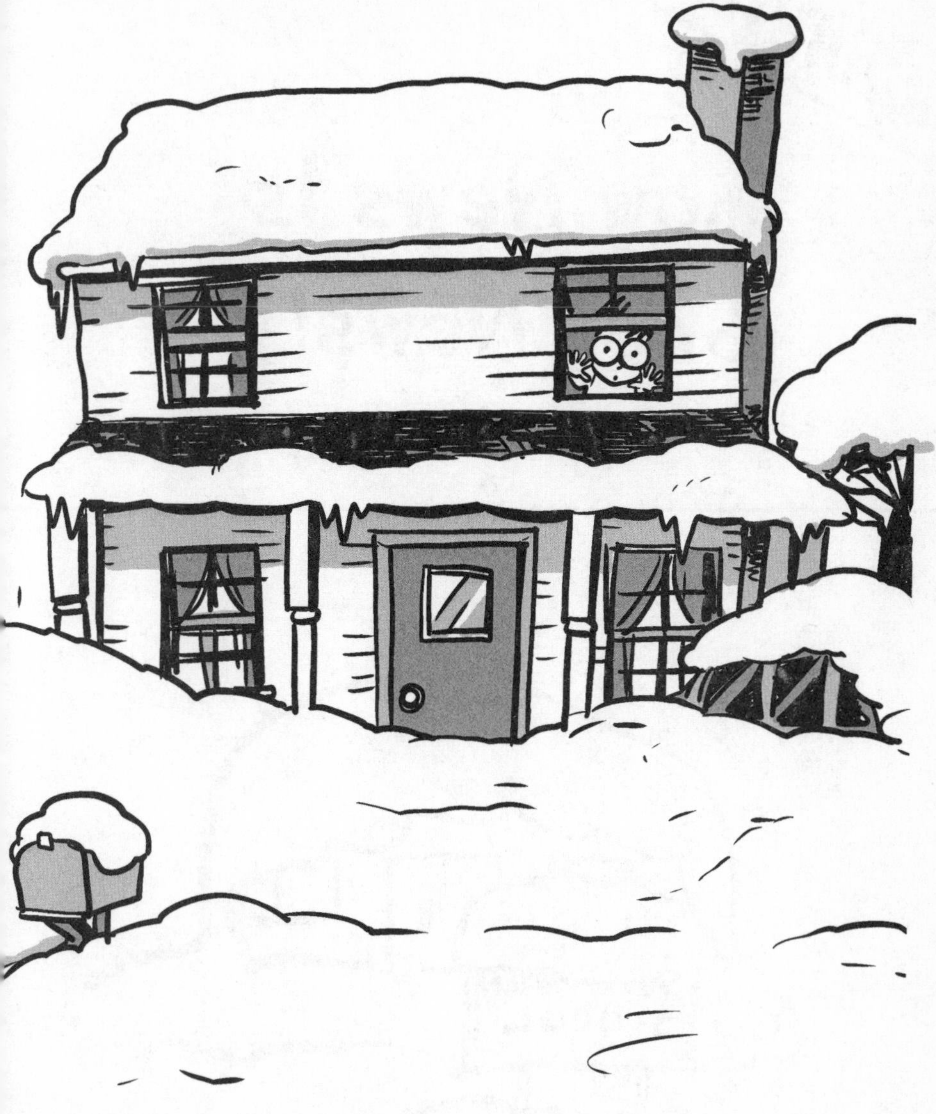

CHAPTER 3

Snow News Is Good News!

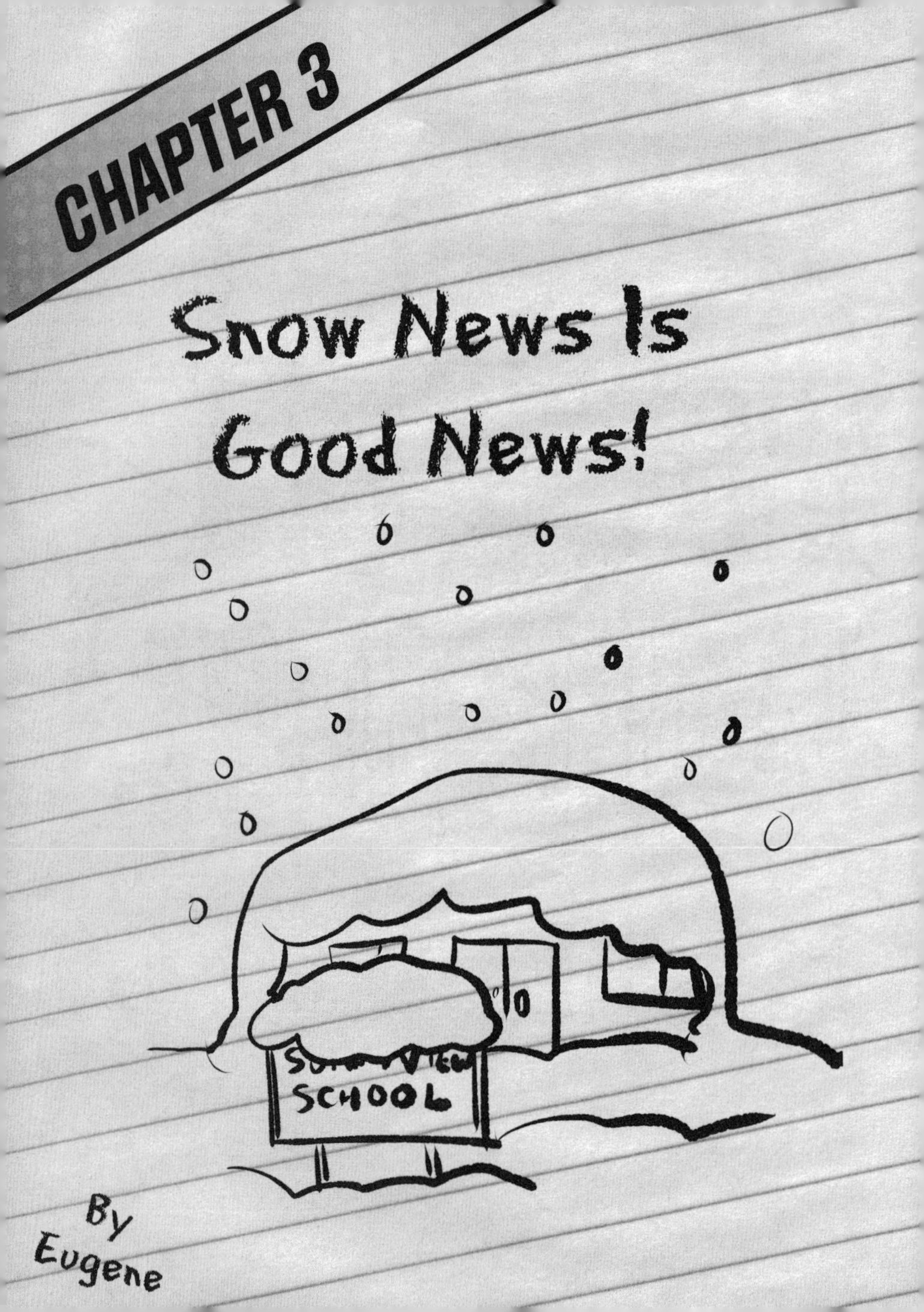
SCHOOL

By Eugene

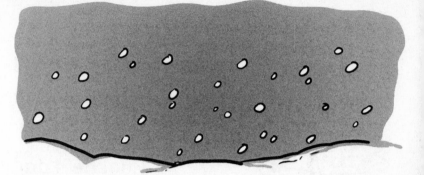

Snow day! It's a snow day! SNOWWWW DAYYYY!" Eugene cheered and ran downstairs, taking the steps two at a time.

"Good morning!" Eugene's mom said cheerily.

"Today's a snow day, right, mom?" Eugene asked, hoping he wasn't still dreaming.

"Yep, it's a snow day. School is officially closed. And not only

that, we're having chocolate-chip pancakes!" Eugene's dad confirmed.

Things just keep getting better! Eugene thought.

There was only one question left to be answered. "Can I invite Charlie and Sally over?" Eugene asked.

"We're already here!" Charlie walked into the kitchen with Sally next to him. "I must have gotten

your brain-wave message that told
me you'd want us to come over."

"And I've been up since six!"
Sally said. "I knew it was going
to be a snow day! I even used my
super speed to shovel my driveway
super speedily!"

"That gives me a great idea," Eugene said.

"We're not going to shovel more driveways, are we?" Charlie asked.

"No," Eugene said. "Are you for-getting who we are?"

"Uh . . . eight-year-old kids?" asked Sally.

"Queen Stinkypants's only friends?" asked Charlie.

"We're superheroes!" Eugene

reminded his friends. "And we're going to spend our snow day doing what superheroes do . . ."

"We're going on patrol!" shouted Charlie and Sally.

"We need to make sure Dr. Yuck Spinach doesn't try to stink up our school with his Leafy Okra Pellets or Lima Bean Traps!" cried Sally.

"We don't have school today," Charlie pointed out. "But maybe Mr. Drools will try to take over the neighborhood with his radio-active drool!"

"But that snow's piled pretty high, even for Mr. Drools," said Sally.

Hmmm . . .

Suddenly, a shadow hopped past the kitchen window and then disappeared.

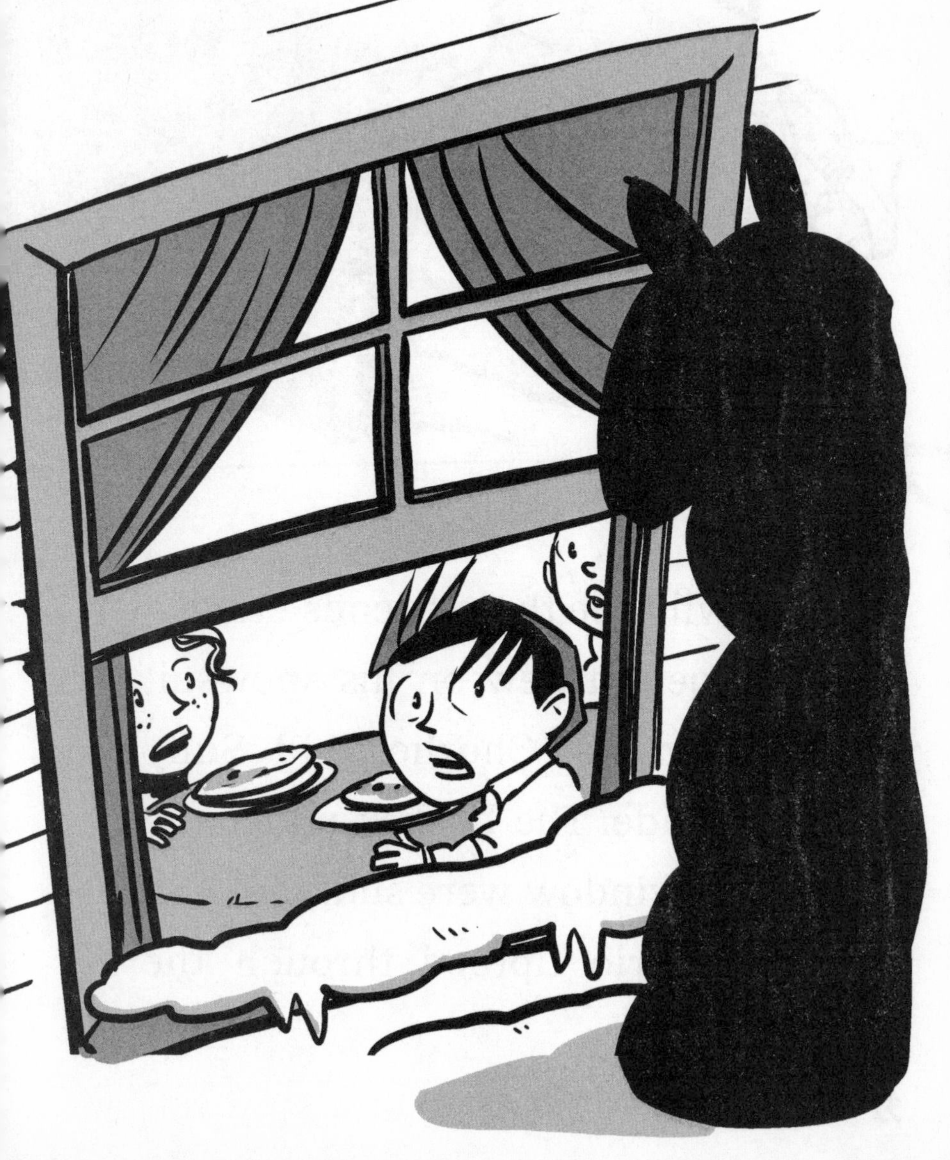

"Evil!" the three friends cried.

Eugene threw on his snowsuit
and then he, Charlie, and Sally
ran outside. The bushes under the
kitchen window were shaking.

The trio tiptoed through the

snow. The bushes shook some more.

"Evil's on the move!" Eugene said.

"It's moving to the front yard," said Charlie.

Eugene, Charlie, and Sally chased the evil creature around the house and arrived just in time to see the creature emerge from the bushes.

"It's a . . . squirrel?" Eugene said.

"And not even an evil alien squirrel or Commander Squirrel and his Acorn Squad," pointed out Sally.

"Just a regular old squirrel," said Charlie.

"Look around, Squad," said Sally.

Eugene and Charlie looked around their neighborhood. The street was covered in snow. No one was walking to work or school or to the store. There were no cars or buses on the road.

"I think even *evil's* taking a snow day today," Sally said.

CHAPTER 4

Calling All Friends

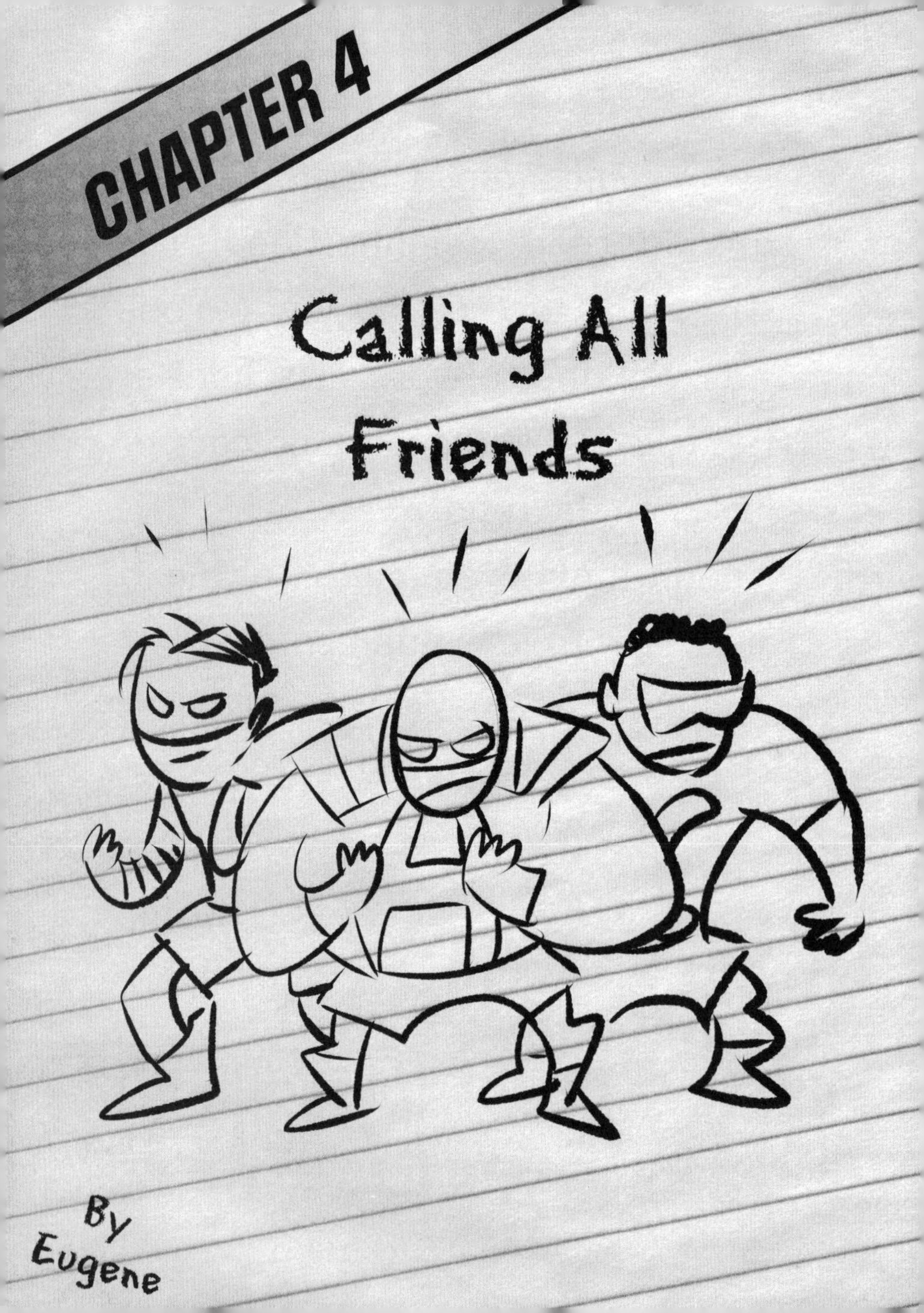

By Eugene

Sorry, guys, but it's too cold out," said Jake Story, still in his pajamas.

Eugene, Charlie, and Sally were standing on the porch at Jake's house. They had decided that if there was no evil to fight, they might as well hang out with their friends, right?

"But it's a snow day," Eugene said.

"And that means it's also an *inside* day," replied Jake.

The trio got the same response all over the neighborhood.

"I'm playing with my new iRobot Dog," said Gil Ditko.

"I'm watching TV," said Neal Chaykin.

"Can't," said Wilma Eisner. "Just started the latest book in the Rider Woofson series."

"Three words," said Dara Sim. "Hot. Chocolate. And marshmallows."

"That's four words," Charlie pointed out.

"And I'm going to enjoy all of them," Dara replied. "Sorry, guys."

The click of the door echoed on the quiet, snow-filled street. On the way back to Eugene's, the members of the Sunnyview Superhero Squad felt defeated . . . and not even by evil! By their friends!

"I can't believe it!" Charlie said. "It's a snow day!"

"It's what we all wanted," Sally added. "I thought the whole point of a snow day was to play outside. In the snow!"

"They don't know what they're missing!" said Charlie. Suddenly, he grabbed a pile of snow in his mittens and rolled it into a ball. Then he put it back down and continued to roll it.

"What are you making, Charlie?" Sally asked.

"The people of Sunnyview will sing songs about what I'm building," Charlie said.

"But what is it?" Eugene asked.

"Easy! It's the bottom part of what's going to be the biggest snow-

man in Sunnyview!" Charlie gave the giant ball of snow a shove. "We just have to find the right place to build the rest of it." The snowball started rolling down the sidewalk.

"Uh, Charlie . . . ," Sally said.

"Look out!" cried Eugene.

The ball was going faster and getting bigger as it picked up more snow. Eugene, Charlie, and Sally raced after it. Sally turned on her

supersonic speed and leaped onto the ball.

She clung on as it kept rolling.

"HELP!" she yelled.

Eugene and Charlie ran to Sally and each grabbed a leg, pulling her from the snowball. The three of them fell backward into the snow.

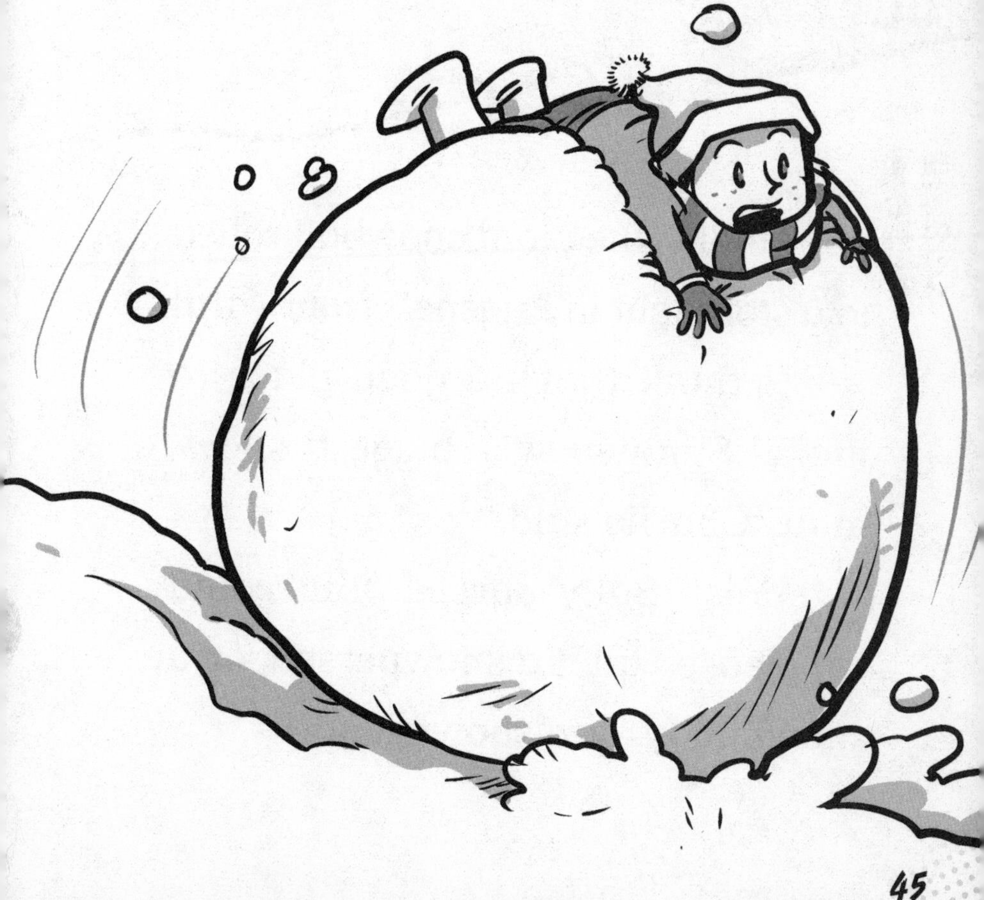

Finally, the giant snowball rolled to a stop right in Eugene's front yard!

"I think that's a good place to make Sunnyview's biggest snowman," Charlie said.

"Yes!" Sally agreed. "But could we please call it a snowperson, or a snowbuddy, or a snowfriend?"

"Good idea!" Eugene said. "Let's build a snowfriend!"

"The *biggest* snowfriend," Charlie reminded them.

Eugene rolled a big snow-ball for its stomach. Sally made a smaller snowball for its head. And Charlie found enough sticks for arms, and rocks to give it a face.

"It's perfect!" said Sally.

"Good work, team," said Eugene.

"Now what?" asked Charlie.

"Hot chocolate break?" Eugene suggested.

The trio raced into Eugene's house without another word.

But if they had stayed outside for a moment more, they might have noticed something odd about the snowfriend.

Was it . . . moving?

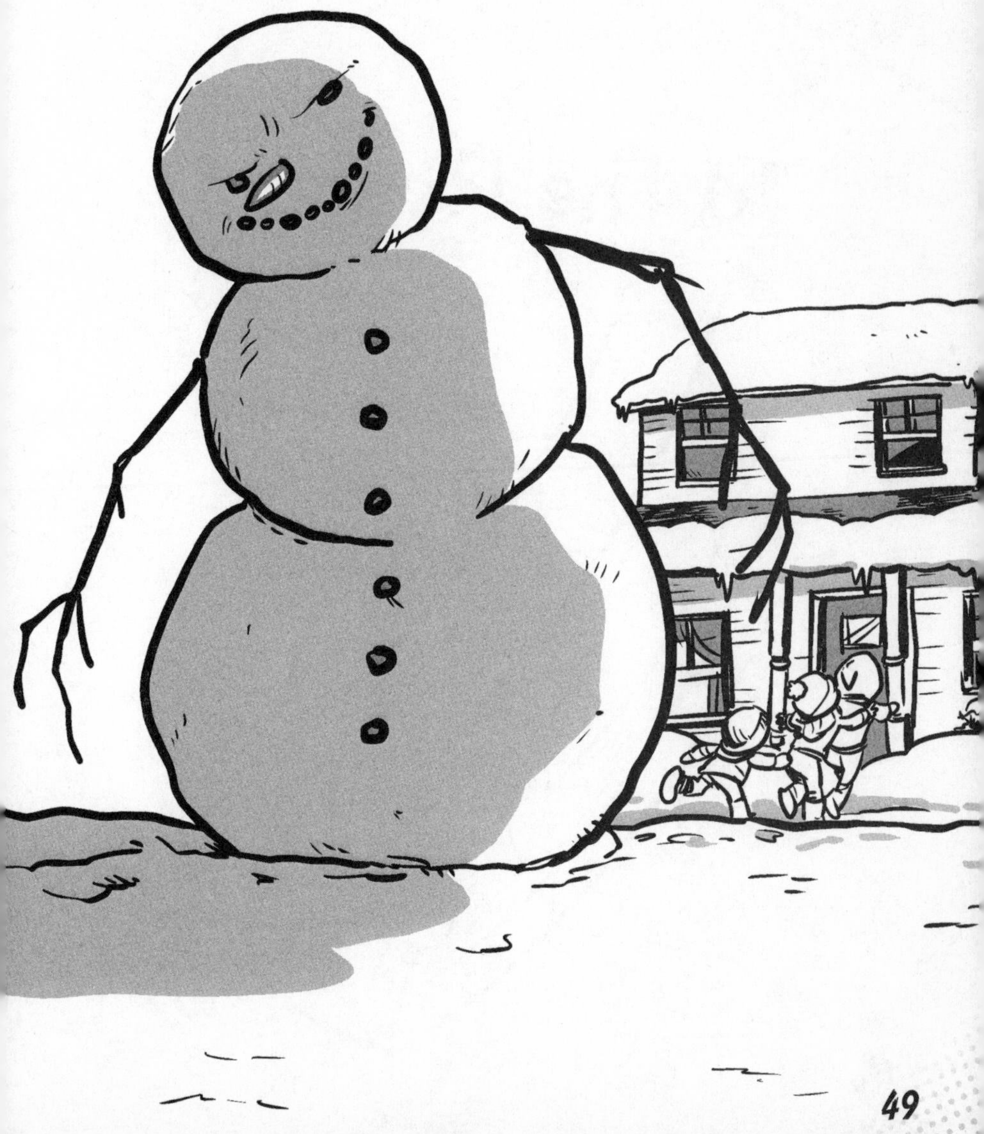

CHAPTER 5

To the Rescue!

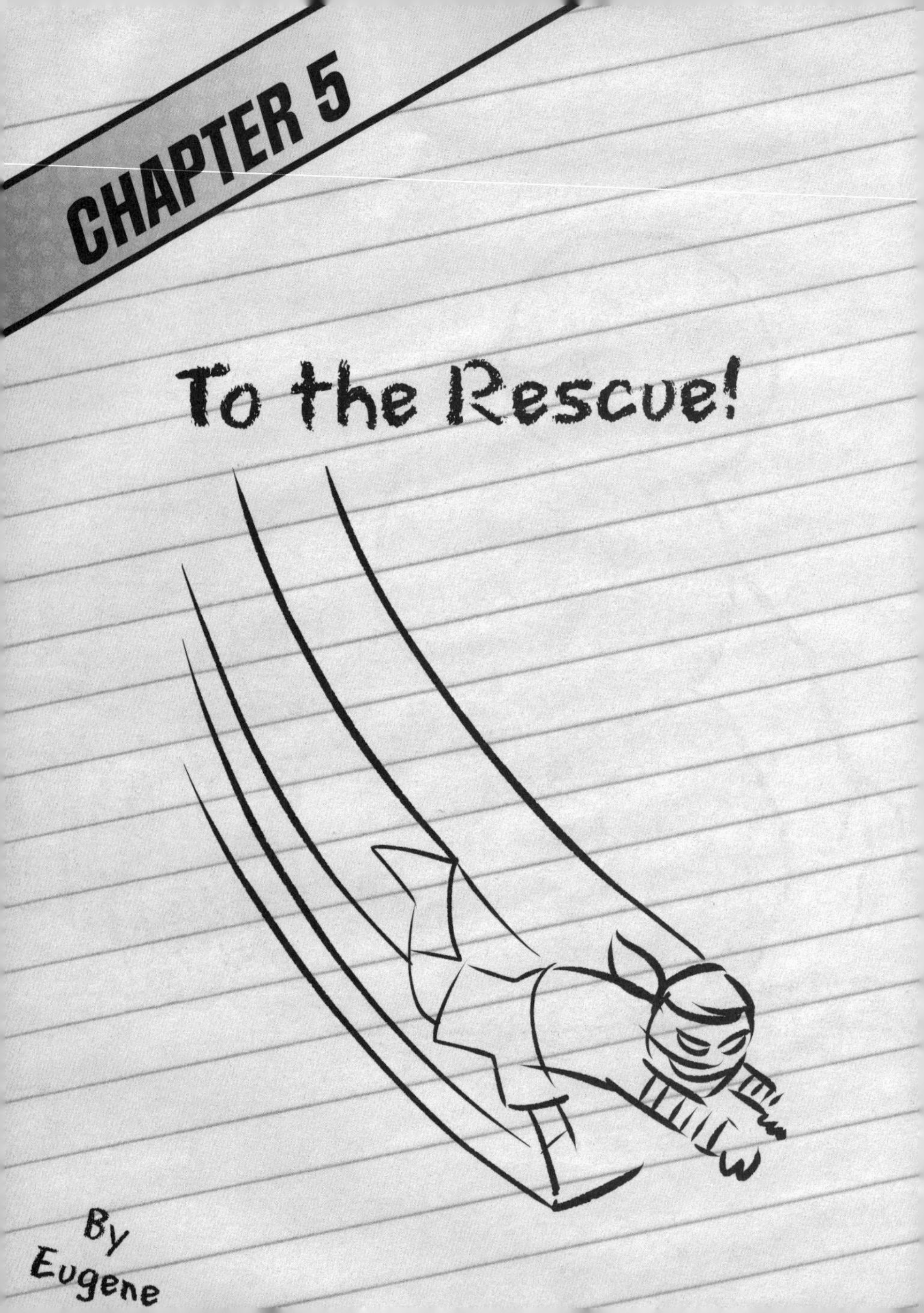

By Eugene

Three cheers for Super Dude's Superhot Chocolate!" Eugene thrust his spoon in the air.

Eugene, Charlie, and Sally were enjoying the best hot chocolate ever as they took a break from snowfriend-building. Charlie would take a sip, then add another marshmallow.

SIP.

MARSHMALLOW.

SIP. MARSHMALLOW.

"Hey, how'd you kids like to go sledding?" Eugene's dad asked as he entered the kitchen.

Eugene hadn't thought

there could be anything better than Super Dude's Superhot Chocolate until . . . SLEDDING!

The three kids bolted for the door.

Ten minutes and thirty-two seconds later, Eugene, Charlie, and Sally raced from the parked car to

Cricket Hill, the best sledding hill in all of Sunnyview.

"I hope everyone from school is here!" Charlie said. "If sledding doesn't get a kid out of the house, nothing will!"

The trio reached the top of the sledding hill and realized that the exact *opposite* of "everyone" was there.

"*No one's* here!" Eugene

gasped. "How is this possible? Are we the only ones who realize that snow equals fun?!"

"Maybe we've been teleported to some crazy backward dimension where kids *hate* snow and *love* school?!" Charlie said, shocked.

"That's not just crazy, that's *evil*!" Eugene cried.

BLAST!

Speaking of evil, the trio was now covered by a wave of snow as someone skidded to a stop directly in front of them.

"My, my, my, if it isn't Eugerm and the dynamic dunces!" Meredith Mooney sneered as she stood from her sled. "Check out my new sled. As if being all pink wasn't awesome enough, it's got a heated seat, cushioned handles, balance gyros, two USB ports, GPS, Bluetooth, *and* a hot chocolate maker." Meredith grabbed a cup of hot chocolate as it popped up from her sled. She took a sip.

"Yummmmmm. So chocolatey," she said.

Eugene looked at his own plastic saucer sled, slightly embarrassed. But he refused to be defeated by Meredith, aka Little Miss Stinky Pinky. "My! Me! Mine! Meredith! I don't care

if your sled makes *doughnuts*—"
Eugene began.

"Oh, it does," Meredith said as
she dipped a glazed doughnut into
her hot chocolate and took a bite.

"Well, we can still beat you in
a race down the hill because these
are . . . FLYING SAUCERS!" Eugene
finished.

"BWAHAHAHAHA!" Meredith laughed so hard, bits of doughnut came out of her mouth. "Flying snotters is more like it. You're on, Eugerm!"

Eugene, Sally, Charlie, and Meredith climbed to the top of the hill, their sleds and saucers tucked under their arms.

"On your marks!" Eugene cried once everyone was seated.

"Go!" Meredith shouted and pushed off.

"Hey! He didn't say 'get set!'" Charlie called out.

But Meredith was already speeding down the hill. There was no way the others could catch up to her.

Then something strange happened. Meredith's sled suddenly veered off to the left.

"What is she doing?" Charlie asked.

"I don't know, but it looks like she might be in trouble," Sally said as they watched Meredith's sled suddenly take a quick turn to the right.

"Heeeeelp!" Meredith cried.

"This is a job for the Sunnyview Superhero Squad!" Eugene yelled.

Eugene, Charlie, and Sally leaped behind a bush.

BACKPACK!
UNZIP!
CAPE!
GOGGLES!
CHEESE!
SUPERHEROES!

Captain Awesome, Nacho
Cheese Man, and Supersonic Sal
jumped onto their sleds and raced
after Meredith.

Captain Awesome used his
cape to give him extra speed. Nacho
Cheese Man shot a burst of Cool
Ranch cheese off the back of his

sled for a boost. And Supersonic
Sal used her own superfast legs to
keep her sled racing forward.

Meredith veered to the left.
Then she veered to the right. Left!
Right! Left! Right!

"Heeeeeeeeeeeelp!" she cried
again.

Supersonic Sal gave herself one last push, then she reached out for Meredith. She grabbed Meredith just in time, and the two of them tumbled into the snow. Captain Awesome and Nacho Cheese Man stopped their sleds next to the girls. Then all four of them watched as Meredith's sled went straight into a bush with a *CRASH!*

"You guys ruined my sled!" Meredith yelled. Then, a little more softly, she said, "But thanks."

"No need to thank the Sunny-view Superhero Squad," said Captain Awesome. "We're just doing our job."

CHAPTER 6

The Frosty Freezing Freezeness of the Frostbiter!

By
Eugene

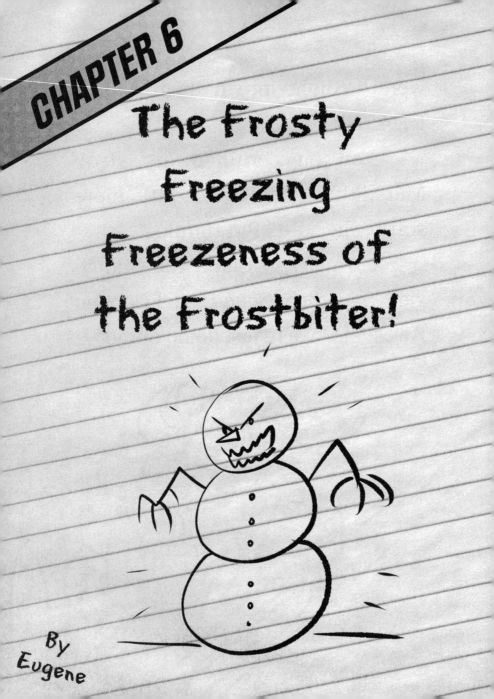

Back at the house, Eugene's dad pulled the car into the driveway.

Eugene, Sally, and Charlie were glad to have helped Meredith at the sledding hill.

After that, the trio had packed away their superhero outfits and done a few more runs on the hill. They had even taken turns giving Meredith their sleds. After all, since there was no evil to fight today,

Meredith wasn't *really* Little Miss Stinky Pinky.

"So . . . what do we do now?" Charlie asked as the kids climbed out of the car.

Eugene thought to himself for a moment.

And then he saw it!

"Into the bushes!" Eugene shouted and tackled Sally and Charlie into a hedge.

"Are we reenacting the scene from Cricket Hill?" Charlie whispered as they peeked out from the bushes, covered in snow.

"No!" Eugene whispered back.

"Look at our snow-friend! He looks . . . *different!*"

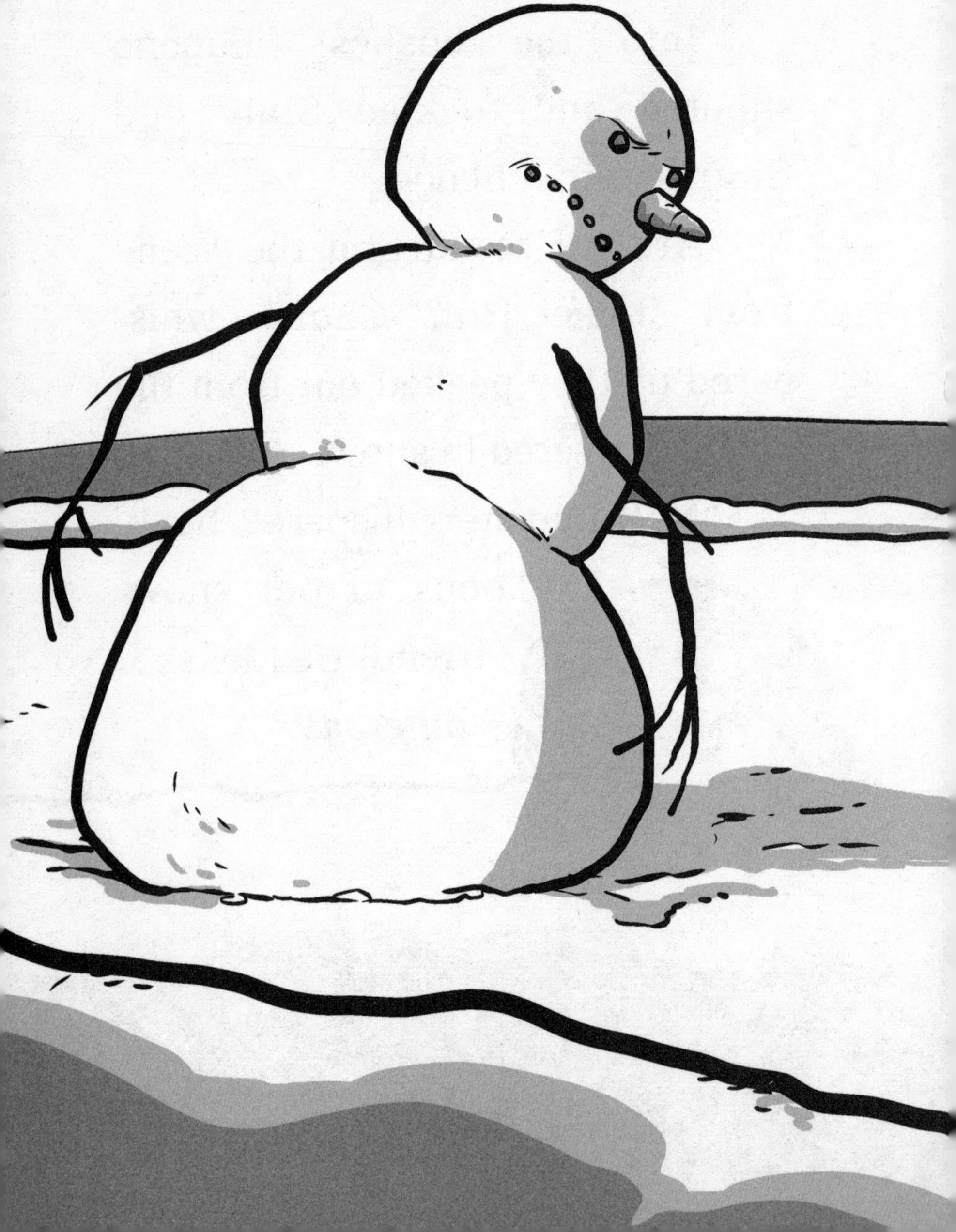

Sally and Charlie stared at the snowfriend.

"Different like less snowy or different like less friendly?" Sally asked.

"Less friendly and more super-villainy!" Eugene replied.

"Hmm . . . ," Charlie said, staring hard. "He *does* look a little meaner now that you mention it."

"A little more frosty," Sally added.

"Guys! That's it!" Eugene gasped. "It's as plain as the snow on the snowfriend's face! That's no ordinary snowfriend! That's the Frostbiter!"

"I'll bet he's sending out evil
brain-freezing
icicle waves
to freeze
everyone's
brains so
they'll hate
snow and stay
indoors!"
Sally cried.
"And that's why
none of our friends will
come out and play!"
Charlie realized.

"And he's here!" cried Eugene. "In my front yard! The freezing-est freeze villain to ever freeze a freezing freeze!"

"To the Sunnyview Superhero Squad's top secret ultra-superhero base!" Sally called out.

CHAPTER 7

The Evilest Thing Evil Ever Eviled!

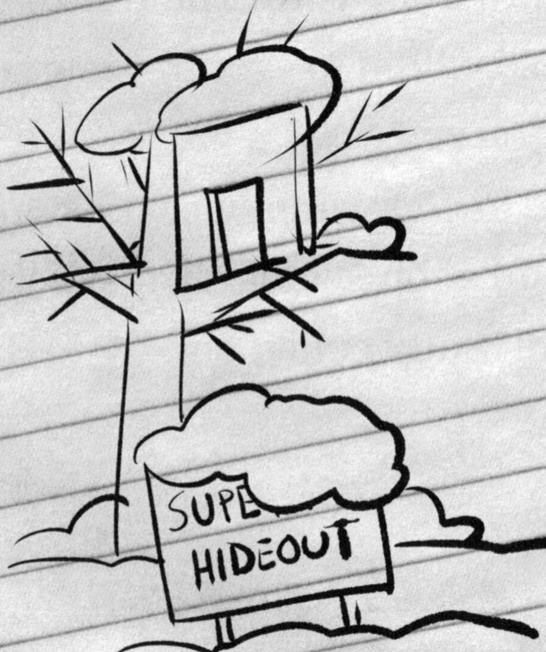
SUPE
HIDEOUT

By Eugene

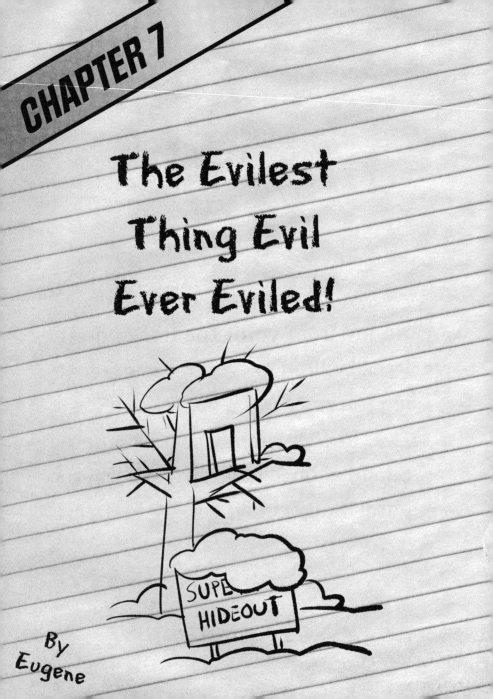

Okay, team. We need a plan,"
Eugene said. He, Sally, and Charlie
were sitting in the tree house in
Eugene's yard that doubled as their
top secret superhero hideout.

"He may be the greatest evil
we've ever faced!" Charlie pro-
claimed. Then he added, "But why
don't we just push him over? His
arms *are* made of sticks."

"We can't *touch* the Frostbiter,"

Eugene explained. "He'll freeze our brains and then *we'll* hate snow, too."

Charlie shuddered at the thought. "It's already getting colder in here," he said.

"So we have to find a way to defeat the Frostbiter without *touching* the Frostbiter," Sally added.

"Yeah. There is no way I'm

giving up my love of snow *or* cheese," Charlie said. "You know, just in case he has those powers, too."

"But if the Frostbiter is freezing everyone's brains, why was Meredith still outside sledding?" Sally asked.

At first Eugene was at a loss for an answer. Then he realized something more horrible than if the comic book store had been sold out of the latest Super Dude issue before he got there.

"It's as plain as the coal in the Frost-biter's eyes!" Eugene said. "Little Miss Stinky Pinky is working with him! She wanted everyone out

of the way so she could sled down Cricket Hill by herself!"

"The only thing worse than having no place to sled is having to wait in line to sled!" Sally said with a gasp. "And with all the other kids staying inside, she had Cricket Hill all to herself!"

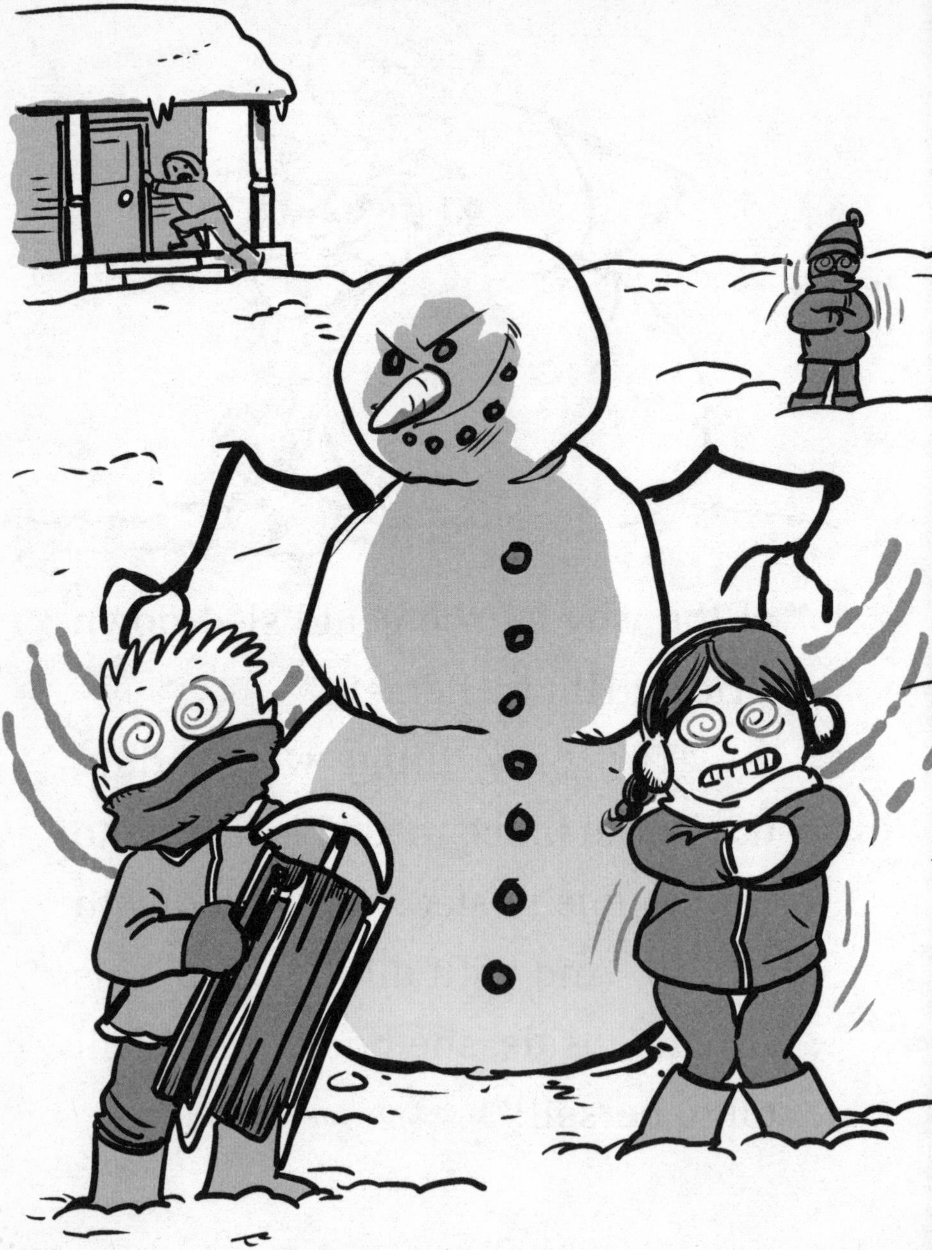

Eugene gasped too. "And what if she purposefully crashed her sled so we'd have to waste time helping her? That just gave the Frostbiter more time to freeze everyone else's brains!" he cried.

"Just when I thought evil couldn't get any more evil, there it goes doing the evilest thing ever eviled," Charlie said.

"Squad, Super Dude didn't fold up his umbrella when the Sand Witches used their super sub sandwich to torpedo his beach picnic in Super Dude No. 99. And we're not

going to give up, either!" Eugene cried.

"What's the plan?" Sally asked.

"We're going to fight snow with snow," Eugene replied. "But first, let's hero up!"

BACKPACKS!
UNZIP!
HERO UP!

Minutes later, Captain Awesome, Supersonic Sal, and Nacho Cheese Man were in their superhero outfits in Eugene's front yard. They snuck into the bushes. Across the yard stood the enemy: the Frostbiter. And in front of them was the ultimate weapon against his brain-freezing icicle waves: the biggest pile of snowballs anyone had ever seen.

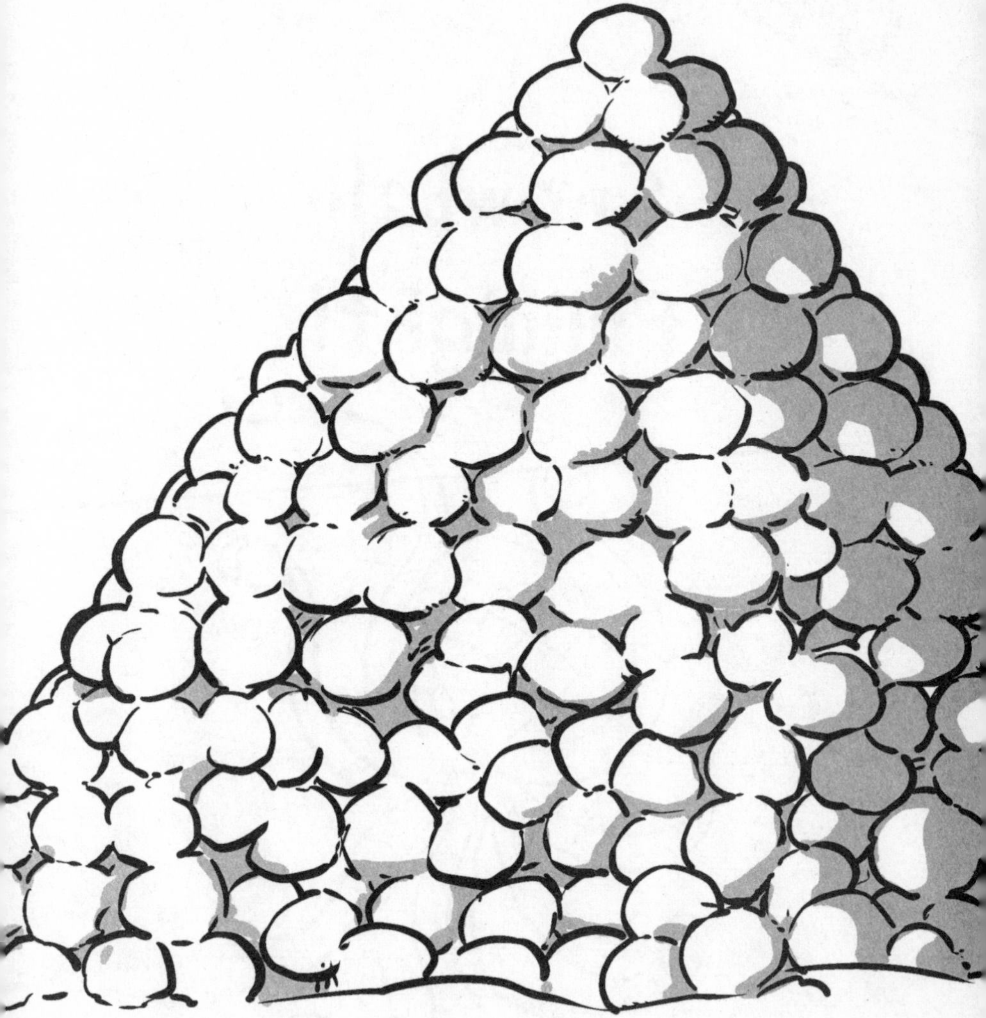

CHAPTER 8

Snowball Fiiiiiiight!

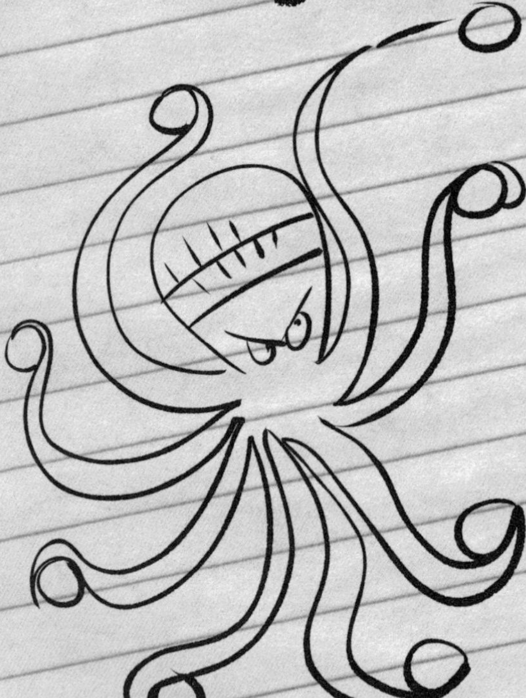

By
Eugene

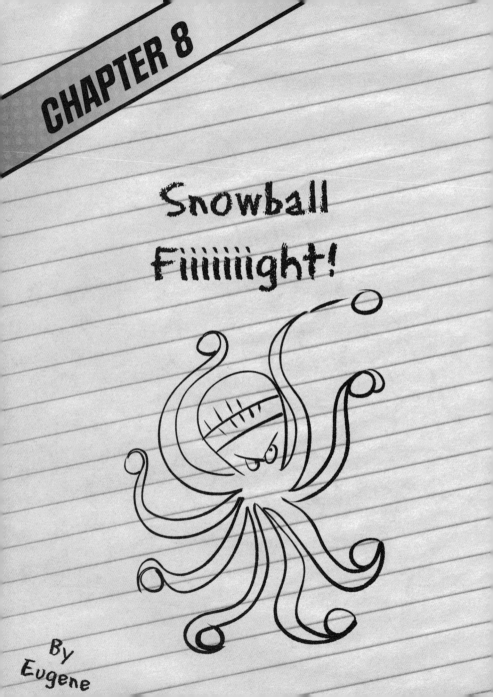

I've got a stack of snowballs that say there's *snow way* the Frostbiter is getting away," Nacho Cheese Man said.

"We may not get out of this without our brains being frozen, so I want to tell you it's been an honor fighting the forces of badness with you," Captain Awesome said to Supersonic Sal and Nacho Cheese Man.

The three heroes gave the Sunnyview Superhero Squad Super Salute and then Supersonic Sal picked up a snowball. "Let's make that lump of snow wish it was summer!" she cried.

Captain Awesome, Nacho Cheese Man, and Supersonic Sal leaped from their hiding place and threw snowballs like they were eight-armed octopuses dressed as superheroes.

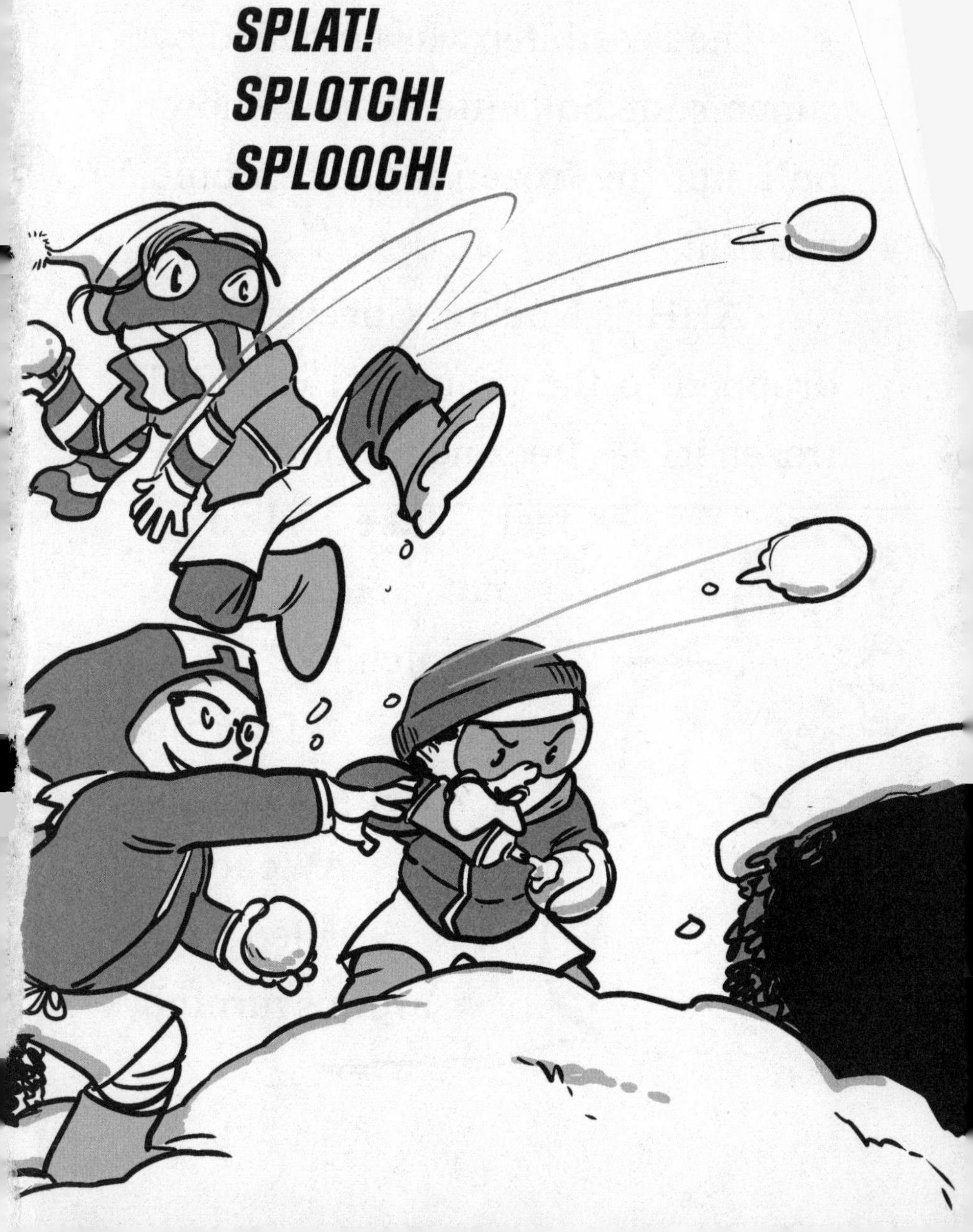
SPLAT!
SPLOTCH!
SPLOOCH!

The Frostbiter was smacked by super snowball after super snowball, but the frozen menace would not fall!

"AHH!" Nacho Cheese Man dropped to the ground. "I can feel frozen icicles freezing my brain! I . . . feel . . . like . . . I've . . . got . . . to . . . go . . . watch TV!"

"Double AHH!" Captain Awesome yelled. "My brain's turning

into an ice cube! Must . . . get . . . inside!"

Supersonic Sal was the only one left! She wound up and let another snowball fly, but it sailed over the Frostbiter and hit someone who was walking by.

And that someone happened to be Meredith Mooney, who was walking home with her older sister, Melissa. Their sleds were tucked under their arms.

"Look out, Meredith! It's a surprise snowball attack!" Melissa laughed. She made a snowball and threw it.

Melissa's snowball plopped down into the snow next to Supersonic Sal, splattering Captain Awesome and Nacho Cheese Man at the same time.

Captain Awesome gasped. "I can feel my brain again! The snow splatter blocked the

Frostbiter's icicle waves!" Captain Awesome cheered.

"That's how we can stop the Frostbiter's brain-freezing icicle waves!" Supersonic Sal said. "We need to have fun in the snow!"

Supersonic Sal grabbed a snowball and

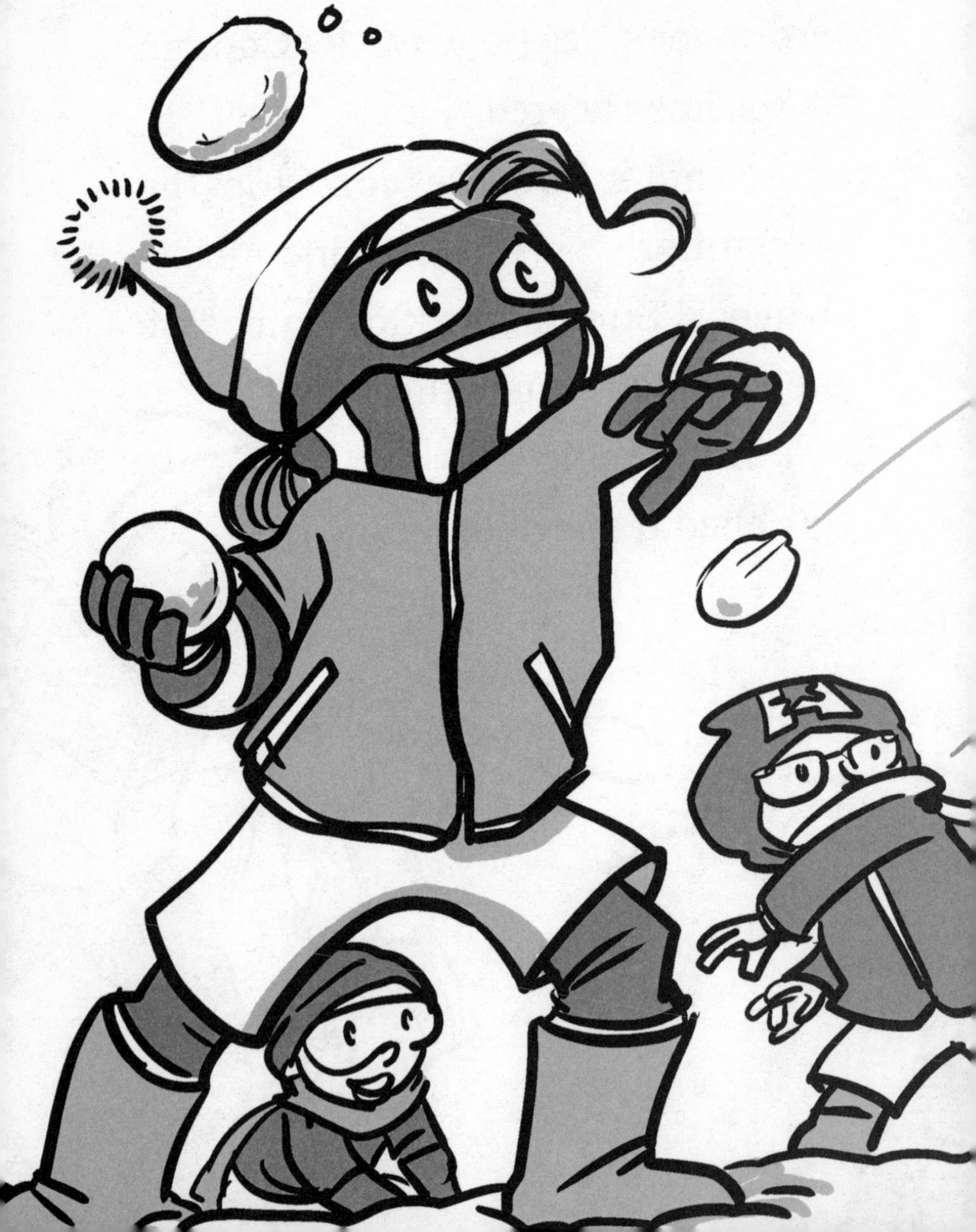

threw it at Melissa, but the snowball missed Melissa and hit Meredith instead. Meredith's face turned pinker than her new sled.

"You did *not* just throw a snowball at me!" Meredith fumed. She made a snowball and threw it wildly. It smacked a laughing Captain Awesome.

Jake Story appeared on the sidewalk. "I saw you guys having a snowball fight from my bedroom window. Can I join in? I love snowball fights!"

"Yeah!" Melissa said and threw

a snowball at him.

Jake Story laughed and threw
one back.

Snowballs flew in all direc-

tions and laughter filled the air.
Within minutes, Wilma Eisner, Olivia
Simonson, Gil Ditko, Neal Chaykin,
Jane Romita, Howard Adams, Ellen

Moore, Stan Kirby Jr., and Dara Sim had joined in the fun!

Snowballs splattered, plopped, and spattered. There were no teams. There was no good versus evil. There was no universe to save or villain to defeat. The TVs would still be there later. So would the video games and the tablets and the computers and the cell phones. But at that moment, they were all a million miles away. Instead, there was just a group of friends . . . and Meredith . . . out in the snow having fun, the way kids were meant to.

And that's just how it should be on a snow day.

CHAPTER 9

A Case of Frozen Identities!

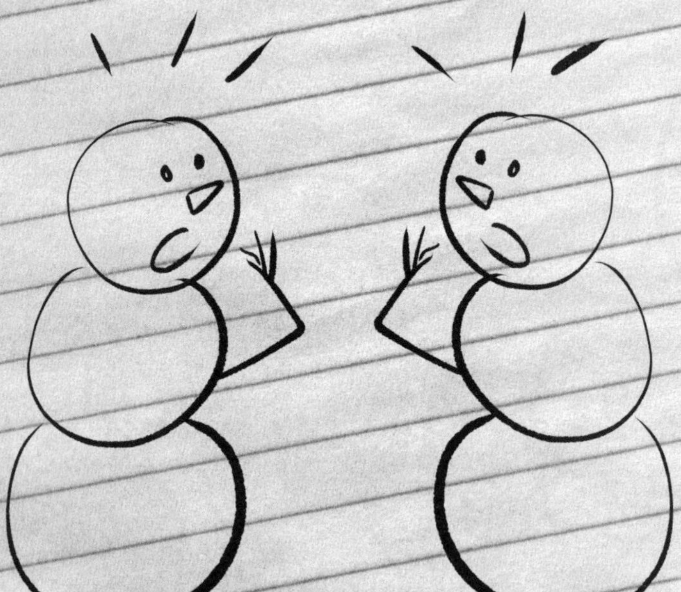

By
Eugene

History would remember it as the Great Sunnyview Snowball Fight, but the kids who ran out from their houses that day to join Eugene, Sally, and Charlie in the snow remembered it as the

MOST SUPER, MOST AWESOME, MOST FUN SNOW DAY EVER!

When the last snowball was thrown, not a single person went

back into their house. Dara Sim and Gil Ditko started making snow angels, while Neal Chaykin, Jane Romita, and others decided to build a snow fort. Wilma Eisner and Howard Adams made more snowfriends, while Stan Kirby Jr. attempted to make an igloo.

And no one was happier than Eugene, Sally, and Charlie.

"The day ended exactly the way we wanted it to start!"

Eugene pointed out. "All our friends ended up outside playing with us after all!"

"Nothing beats a good snowball fight!" Sally added.

"And we owe it all to the Frostbiter!" Charlie realized. "If we hadn't tried to blast him back to the North Pole with snowballs, none of this would have happened."

"Which kind of makes him a . . .

good guy?" Sally asked, unsure.

"Guys! It all makes sense now!" Eugene pointed at the snowfriend. "That's not the Frostbiter! That's his superhero cousin, Captain Freezy McFreeze!"

"You mean this was all a case of frozen identity?" Charlie gasped.

"We owe him an apology," Sally said.

The trio gave Captain Freezy McFreeze a Sunnyview Superhero Salute.

"Sorry for trying to blast you back to the North Pole with

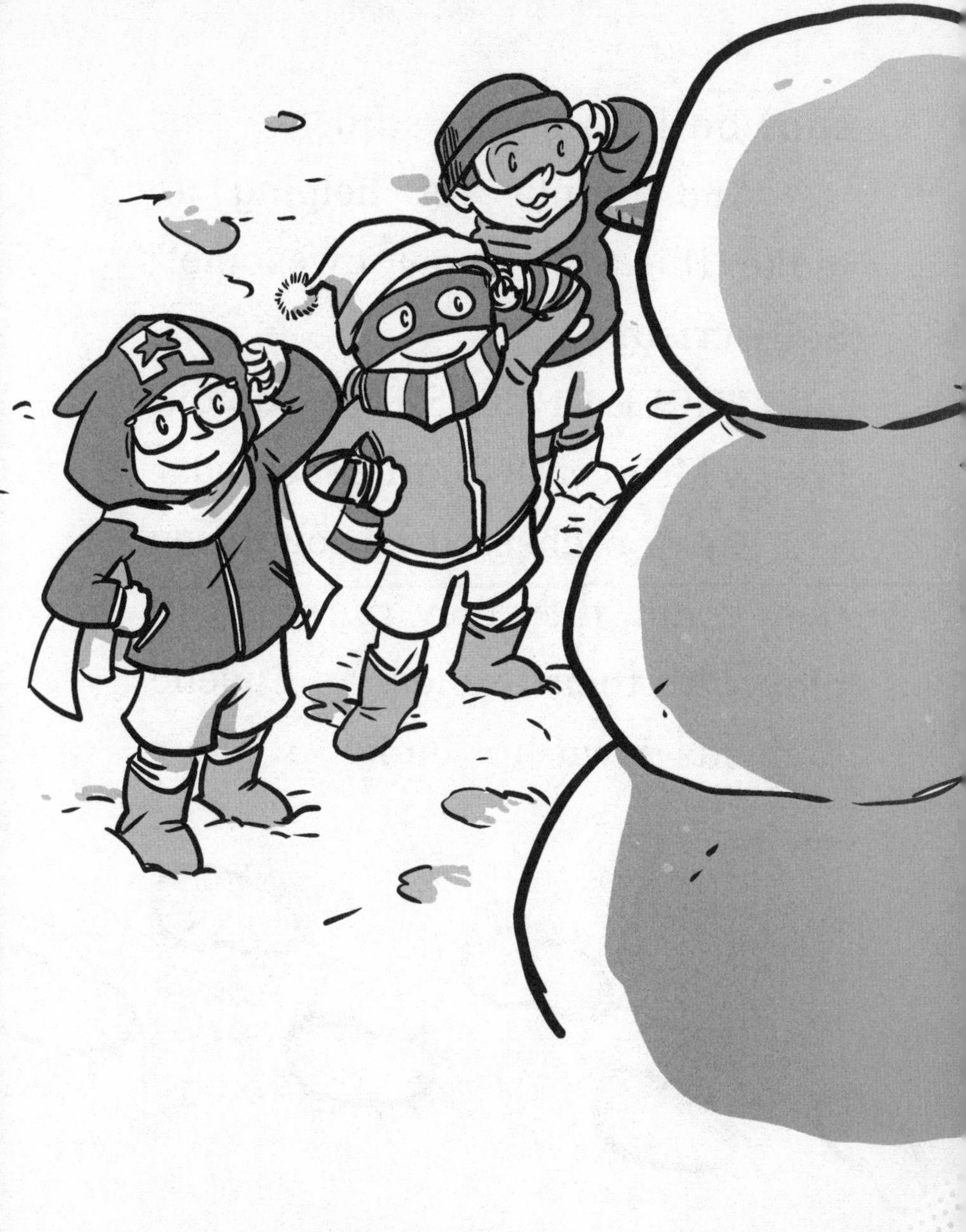

snowballs," Eugene said.

"And thanks for helping us make this day *snow* awesome!" Sally cried.

"THREE CHEERS FOR Captain Freezy McFreeze!" Charlie shouted.

The trio cheered as loudly as they could, then they raced off to play with their friends. As Eugene flopped down to make a snow

superhero next to Ellen Moore's
snow angel, he could only think of
one word to describe the day . . .
MI-TEE!

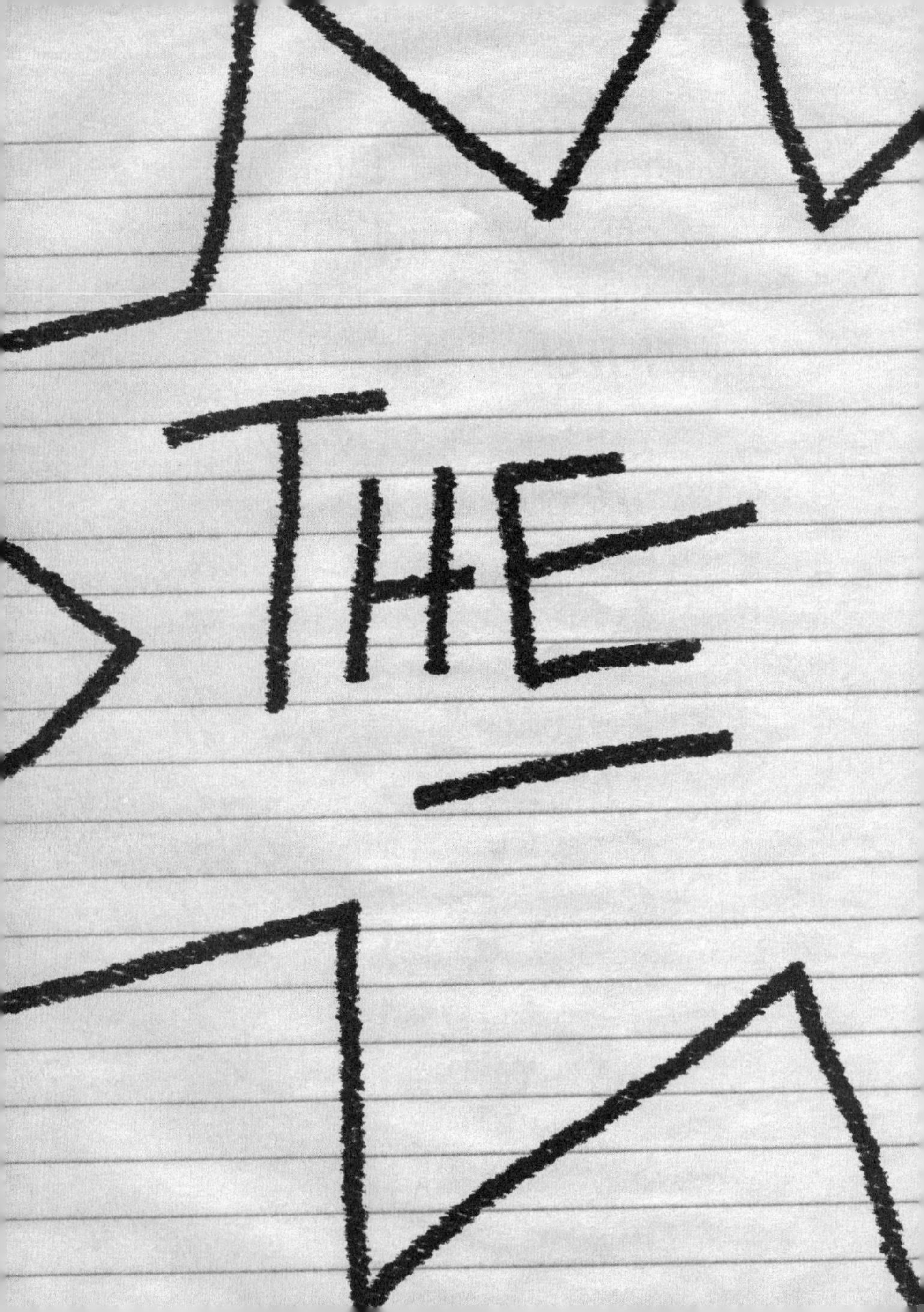
THE

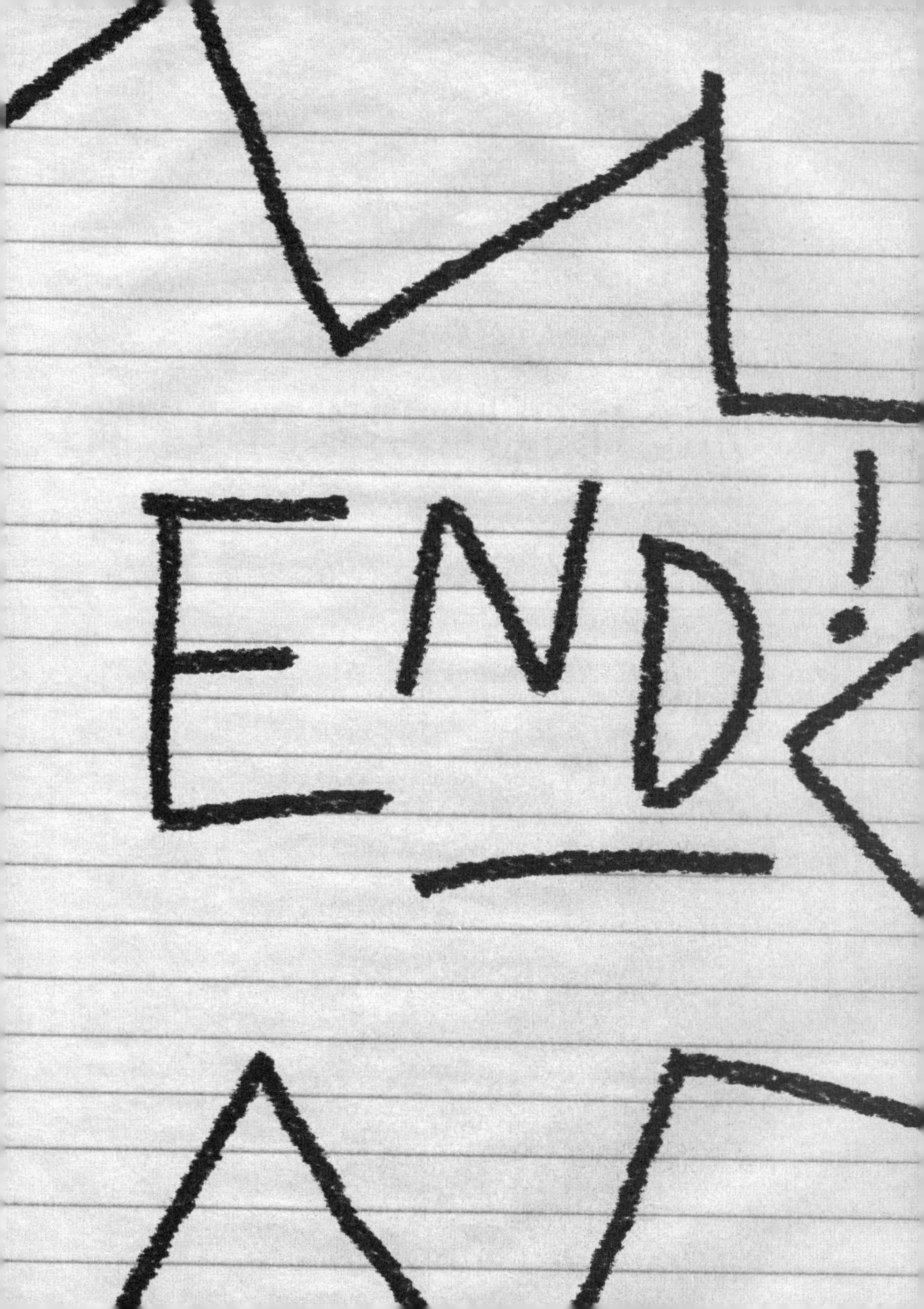
END!

MEANWHILE, AT SUNNYVIEW ELEMENTARY

BEHOLD: SUNNYVIEW ELEMENTARY
SCHOOL! INSIDE THESE WALLS
THERE IS A BIG SECRET!

SUNNYVIEW
ELEMENTARY

But for now it was perfectly quiet at Sunnyview Elementary. No kids running down the halls, no teachers giving out pop quizzes, no second-grade students reaching into Turbo's cage—

Oh, who's Turbo, you ask? He's this little guy here.

If you couldn't guess, Turbo is a hamster. His fur is mostly white, but he has a big brown spot on his back. He has little pink ears and buck teeth.

And this—er—palace is Turbo's home. Here in the corner of Ms. Beasley's second-grade class.

Turbo, you see, is the official pet of Sunnyview Elementary's Classroom C.

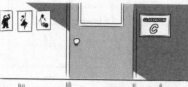

And even on a day like today, when the school was closed for snow, Turbo took his job as classroom pet very seriously.

He made sure to do all his regular classroom pet things.

He drank some water. *GLUG,
GLUG, GLUG.*

He ate some pellets. *MUNCH,
MUNCH, MUNCH.*

And he ran on his hamster wheel.
SQUEAK, SQUEAK, SQUEAK.

When he was finished, only a few

minutes had passed. Now what? Usually Turbo liked when the kids went out to recess and he got some peace and quiet. But today it was almost *too* quiet.

Suddenly, it wasn't quiet anymore. Turbo was sure he heard a rustling coming from the cubbies.

Straining his tiny ears, Turbo listened as hard as he could.

"There is definitely something there," Turbo said to no one in particular. "I'm the official pet of Classroom C, and so it is my duty to find out the source of this mystery sound!"

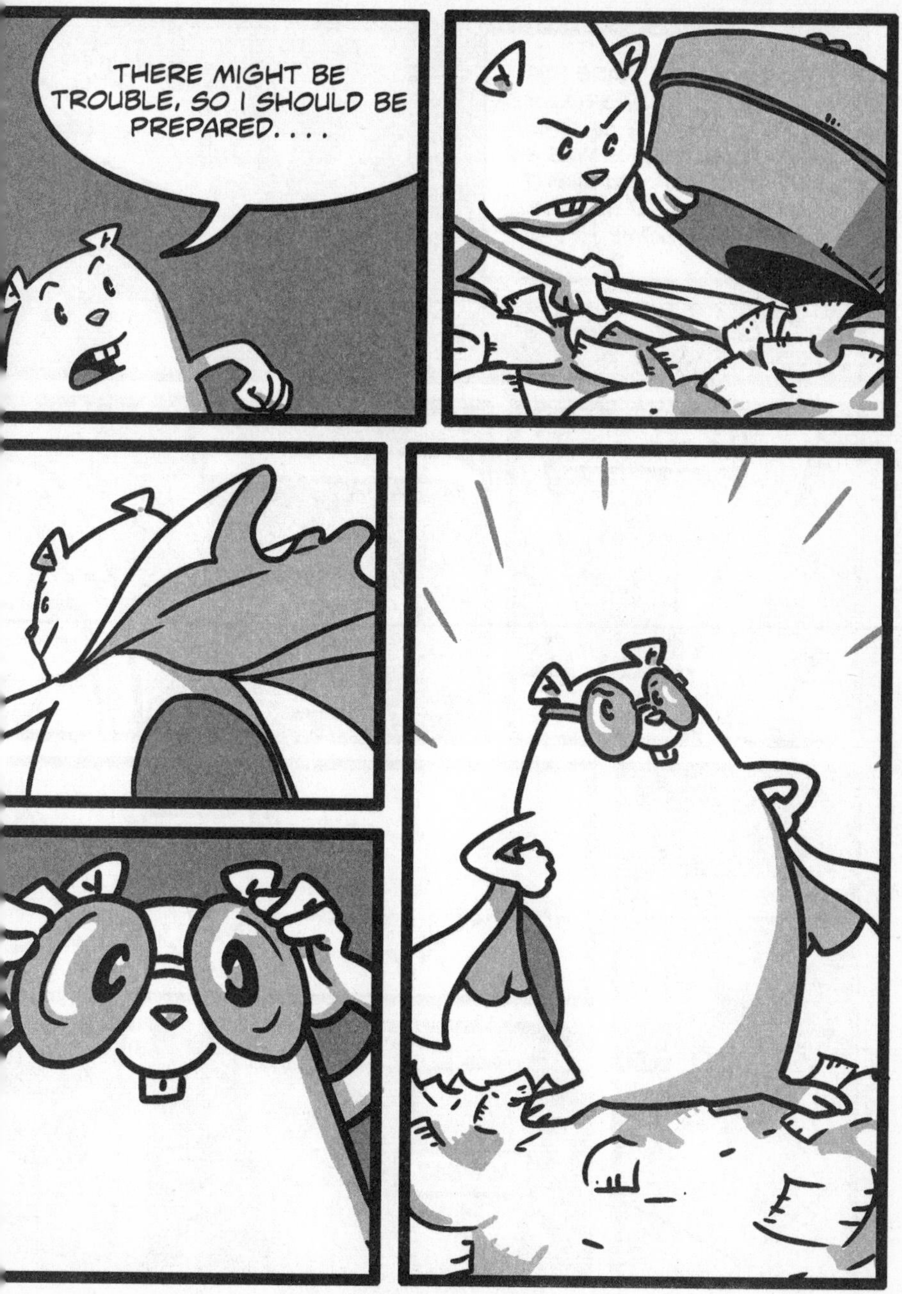
THERE MIGHT BE TROUBLE, SO I SHOULD BE PREPARED. . . .

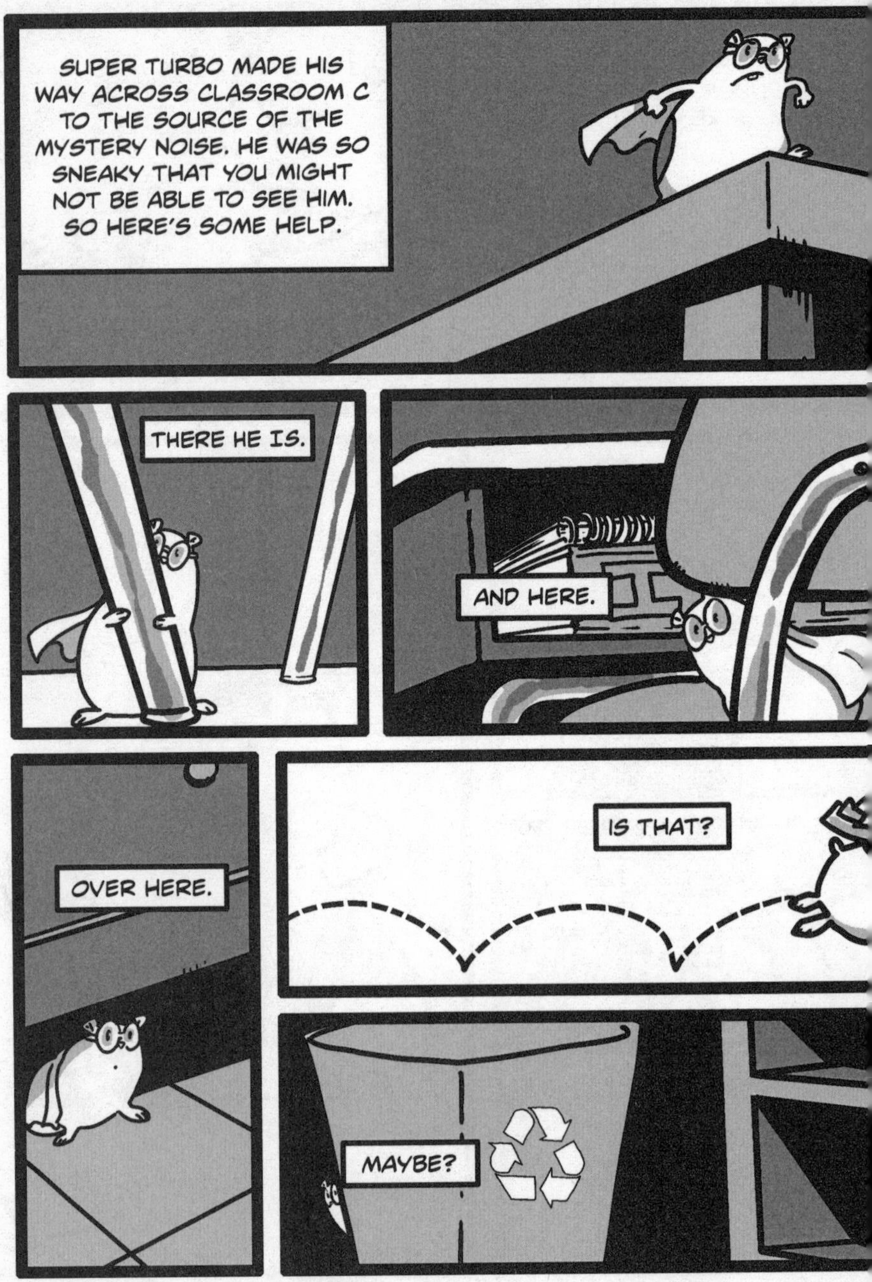
SUPER TURBO MADE HIS WAY ACROSS CLASSROOM C TO THE SOURCE OF THE MYSTERY NOISE. HE WAS SO SNEAKY THAT YOU MIGHT NOT BE ABLE TO SEE HIM. SO HERE'S SOME HELP.
THERE HE IS.
AND HERE.
OVER HERE.
IS THAT?
MAYBE?

Finally, Turbo got to where the noise seemed to be coming from. And then he saw a tail and it belonged to a terrible, awful, frightening . . .

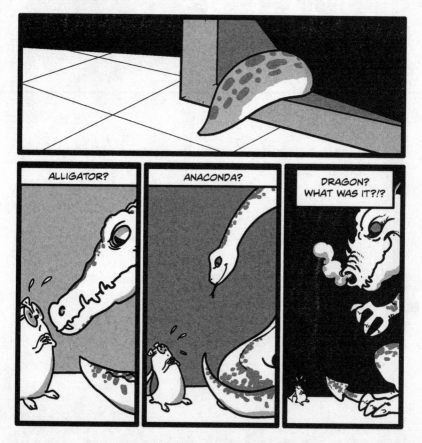

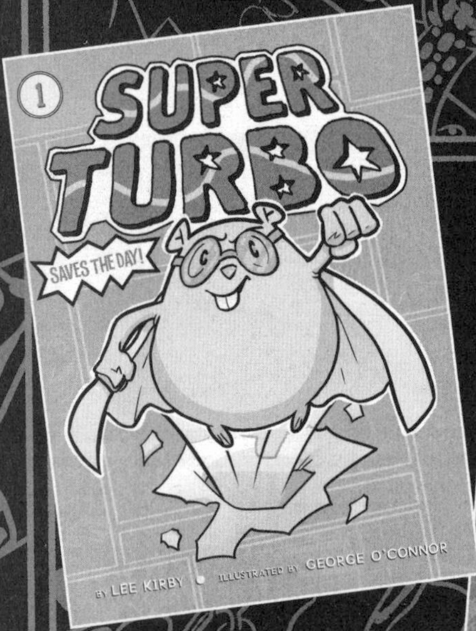
1
SUPER TURBO
SAVES THE DAY!
BY LEE KIRBY
ILLUSTRATED BY GEORGE O'CONNOR

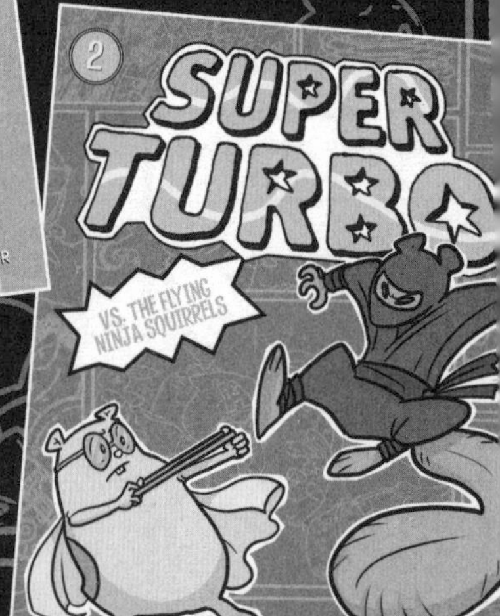
2
SUPER TURBO
VS. THE FLYING NINJA SQUIRRELS
BY LEE KIRBY
ILLUSTRATED BY GEORGE O'CONNOR